CABIN FEVER

by Norma Linsenman-Schuh

Illustrated by
Dennis Rogers

A Happy To Be Me® Book
Esteem International, Inc.
Eden Prairie, Minnesota

*T*o all children throughout the world in celebration of the special people they are, with the hope that they will become all they can be.

To our own children — Bryce, Cirée, Marc, Vicky, Jeff, Karna, Eric, Calley, Collin, Jeffrey, John, Steve and Lynn — for the unique opportunity they gave us to experience the magic of parenting, and to our parents for the loving role models they provided us as children.

The Esteem International Team

Happy To Be Me is a registered trademark of **Esteem International, Inc.**
Text and Illustration Copyright 1993 **Esteem International, Inc.**
Library of Congress Catalog Card Number 93-72990
All rights reserved.

No part of this book may be reproduced or transmitted in any form or by any means, electronic or mechanical including photocopying, recording, or by any information storage and retrieval system, without permission in writing from the publisher.

For information contact: **Esteem International, Inc.**

Printed and bound in the United States of America
First edition, 1993.

*A*li walked to the living room window and watched the snow blow across the road. Huge white flakes had been falling for days, covering everything in sight.

The Marinos
had been stuck
inside since
Tuesday. Ali
thought the
storm was beautiful,
but not everyone agreed.

"There's NOTHING to do,"
complained Bryan. He tossed a sofa
pillow at Andy, just for some excitement.
Her two brothers were at it again.

"Cut it out, gerbil face!" Andy shouted, as he lunged
toward Bryan.

"Make me, chicken lips!" Bryan yelled back.

"Settle down you two!" Mrs. Marino warned, "or you'll wind up in your rooms!" She stepped between her two sons to stop them from fighting.

"*I* think we all have cabin fever," Ali's grandma said, looking up from her crossword puzzle. She was right. It was too cold to go outside. Too cold to skate or slide. Even Max, Ali's dog, for once wasn't begging at the door to be let out. School had been cancelled and the stores were all closed.

It seemed as if they'd been inside forever!

"Why don't you boys play ping pong downstairs," Mrs. Marino suggested, trying to think of something to keep them busy.

"I'm tired of games," said Bryan, as he prepared to shoot a rubber band at Andy.

"And I'm sick of TV," said Andy, stretching out on the couch.

Grams yawned and took off her glasses. "I've had enough of this puzzle for one day," she said, closing her book in her lap.

"I'm tired of this too," Mrs. Marino said, putting her novel down beside her.

"Alioop, what are you doing out there?" Grams called out, noticing Ali had disappeared from the room.

Happy To Be Me

"*I* just frosted the brownies I baked this morning," Ali said, bouncing back from the kitchen. "Anybody want one?" she asked, offering the plate to Grams. "Woof!" barked Max. He sat up on his hind legs and pawed the air. Ali stooped down, putting her arms around his neck.

"You know chocolate makes you sick!" she said, "but I've got something even better for you." She went to the kitchen and came back with a rawhide bone. "There you go, Mr. Max," Ali said, leaning down to kiss his black leathery nose. She didn't want him to be left out.

$\mathcal{A}$li had planned on going to her room to paint a glow-in-the-dark picture on her sweatshirt. She was in a creative mood. *After that, maybe I'll make up a song on my keyboard or write a poem,* she thought.

With so many fun things to do, Ali didn't have time to be bored. The days were never long enough for her. Even when it was freezing cold. Even during a snowstorm. She could always think of something exciting to do.

But Ali knew Grams and Mom were restless, and she was pretty sure that Bryan and Andy would start arguing again as soon as all the brownies were gone. *Instead of painting or composing,* she decided, *I'd better think of something the whole family can do together. Maybe we could do face painting or take weird pictures of each other. What would be fun for all of us?* she wondered. Ali lay on the floor thinking, as Grams gently tapped her pencil on her book. Tap... Tap...Tap...TAP! TAP!

"Grams," Ali said, looking excited, "you've given me a great idea! Let's have a talent show, and you can show us all how you used to tap dance!" Grams' eyes lit up, and Bryan lifted one eyebrow. This could be interesting.

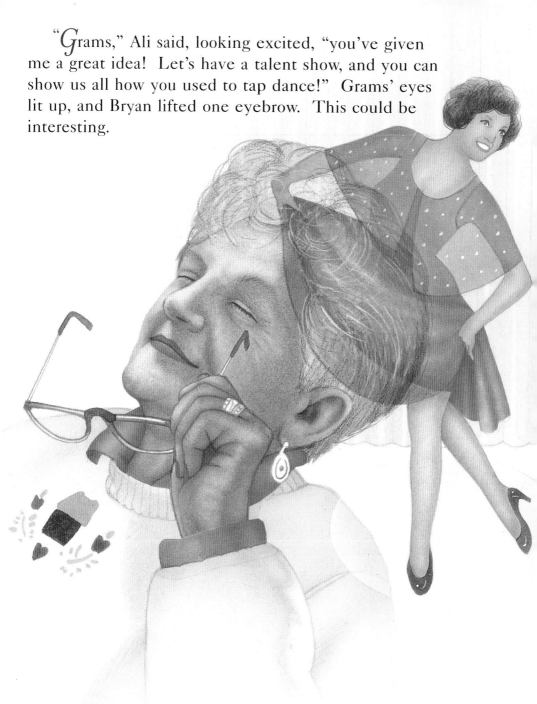

He'd seen a photo of Grams in a theater costume but had never seen her dance. Besides, Bryan was a ham and liked having an audience as much as Ali did.

"*I* think that would be a hoot!"
Ali's mom said, getting up
from her chair.

"Let's say we all have one hour to come up with an act and put together a costume. Everybody in the family room at one o'clock sharp!" Ali shouted. "Last one back has dog breath!" she said, running down the hall. Everyone disappeared. They had forgotten all about the snowstorm and being stuck inside.

13

*A*li quickly cleared the furniture from one end of the family room to make a small stage.

She hung an old blue-and-white quilt from the mantle to make a back drop. "I'll set up chairs for the audience," said Andy, dragging in six of them from the dining room.

"We'll have to be both the actors and the audience!" Ali said, laughing. She loved to organize things, and she was good at it.

"*H*ere, make some tickets out of these," she said to Bryan, handing him some gum wrappers from the candy dish on the table. "Do five," she said. "No, make that six," she decided. "Max needs one too."

Grams found two flashlights to use as spotlights, and Mrs. Marino carried in a giant bowl full of buttered popcorn for the audience to munch on during the show.

Ali dashed to her room and came back with two posters. She tacked them up on the quilt for decoration.

"The theater is ready," she announced. "Now all we need are the stars!"

"And costumes," reminded Grams. Everyone hurried off in a different direction in search of something to wear.

aristide
BRUANT

*A*li went to the closet in the spare bedroom where her mom stored clothes and holiday decorations. She had no idea what she could do for her act. Turn down the lights and tell a scary story? Make shadow animals on the wall?

On the shelf above all the hangers, Ali spotted a hat box with fuchsia feathers peeking out of it. *Grams' boa from the Halloween party!* she thought excitedly, grabbing the box and taking off the cover. *I can be a famous entertainer — a singing star!* She flipped through the hangers, looking for the rest of her costume.

$\mathcal{A}$li knew just what she needed — the shimmery rose-colored dress her mother had worn on Valentine's Day for the grand opening of the art gallery she owned. Reaching to the far end of the cluttered closet, she felt the slippery fabric of the dress and pulled it out. It sparkled like diamonds and was just as beautiful as she'd remembered.

*A*ll she needed now was some music. *My tape of French songs will be perfect!* Ali thought, hurrying to her room. She'd listened to it so many times, she knew all the words by heart. Humming her favorite tune, Ali found the tape in her "Special Box" under her bed and popped it into her tape player. She dressed quickly, slipped on a pair of shoes, and headed for the family room with three minutes to spare.

𝒷ryan and Andy were already there. They'd tied matching bathtowels around their necks for capes. And both of them wore sparkling white hats they'd made out of cardboard and glitter.

"Who are you supposed to be?" Bryan asked his sister, as she made her grand entrance. "Bonjour, monsieur ... My name eez Monique," Ali said, trying to sound French, as she tossed her boa over her shoulder.

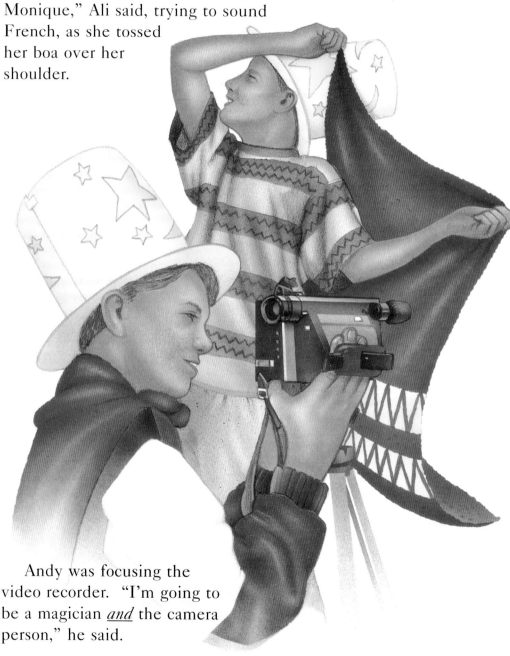

Andy was focusing the video recorder. "I'm going to be a magician *and* the camera person," he said.

Grams had on the fancy dress she'd worn for her sixty-fifth birthday party. On her feet were the same shiny black shoes Bryan had seen in the old photo. "I may have grown a little wider since I was young," Grams said laughing, "but my feet are still the same size!"

"Howdy do, y'all!" Mrs. Marino said, coming down the stairs. She was wearing a blond Halloween wig, one of Bryan's old straw cowboy hats, knee-high snow boots, and she was strumming a guitar. All over her outfit, she'd wrapped gold drapery fringe.

"This ought to be great," Grams laughed, "a real live country western star!"

Ali flipped the lights on and off to signal the show was about to begin. Grams went to the entrance and took tickets.

When everyone was seated, Bryan ran to the stage and waited for Grams to shine the spotlight on him. He talked into a turkey baster as if it were a microphone. "Ladies and gentle*man*, and you too, Max," he said. "Welcome to the greatest show of the century! Our first act features a famous musician, my mom!"

$\mathcal{A}$li's mom stepped on stage, strummed her guitar and sang "Home on the Range." When she finished, everyone clapped and cheered. Then Bryan announced the world famous dancer, "Grams Marino." Tapping her heels against the wooden floor, Grams went from one side of the room to the other. Max followed her, barking at the noise. She bowed gracefully at the end of her act, and everyone applauded loudly. The boys whistled their approval through their fingers.

aristide
Bruant

When it was Andy's and Bryan's turn, Ali took charge of the video camera. Bryan started the magic act by showing the audience Andy's empty hat. Then he swung it through the air and pulled a pair of his underwear out of it. "Way to go!" Ali yelled, acting like she didn't see him sneak the underwear from inside his sleeve.

Then Bryan got into a box, and Andy pretended to saw it in half with a butter knife while Bryan filed his nails and hummed non-chalantly. After a few more tricks, it was Ali's turn.

She pressed the start button on her tape player, ran to the stage and pretended to sing the song on the tape. As she moved her lips in time to the words, she flung her boa around her neck dramatically.

Max walked over to the stage and sat down next to Ali. He looked up at her quizzically and tipped his head to the side.

Suddenly he threw his head back and HOWLED right in time with the music.

"What a team!" Grams yelled. "Hey, Max," Bryan teased, "you need a new singing partner!"

$\mathcal{E}$veryone laughed and clapped. The more commotion they made, the more Max sang!

Ali wrapped the boa around Max so he had a costume too, and Bryan put his magician's hat on Max's head. Everyone howled with laughter, including Ali, who could hardly finish her act. When the song was over, Ali scooped Max into her arms and they bowed together.

"My stomach hurts from laughing so hard," Mrs. Marino said, wiping tears from her eyes.

"I'd like to do it all over again," Grams said, still chuckling.

"I have a better idea," Bryan volunteered. "Let's watch ourselves on TV!" Andy popped the video tape into the VCR.

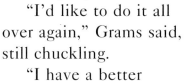

The talent show rolled before them, and everyone laughed all over again.

"We're really good!" Grams said when it finished.

"Hey, look outside!" Ali shouted. "The snow's stopped and there's something bright in the sky!" Bryan and Andy ran to the window just as the sun peeked out from behind a winter-gray cloud.

"Let's get our saucers and slide down the hill," Bryan shouted, excitedly.

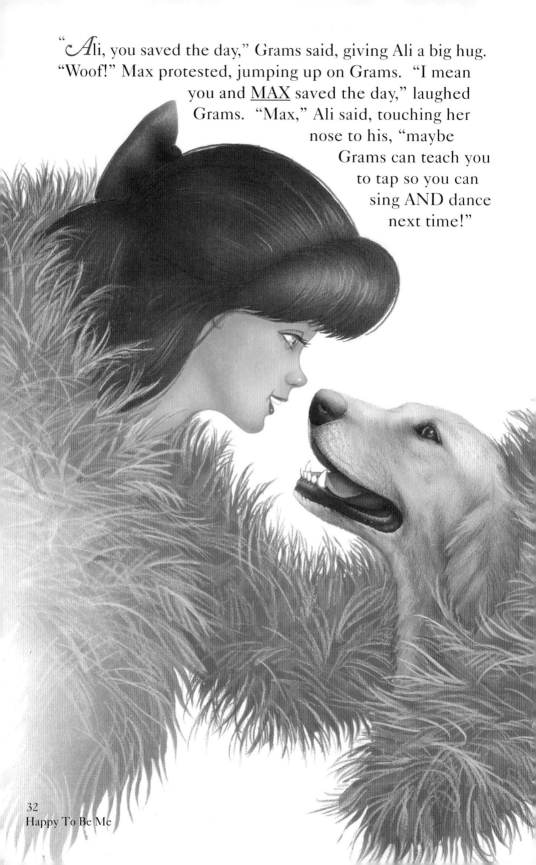

"Ali, you saved the day," Grams said, giving Ali a big hug. "Woof!" Max protested, jumping up on Grams. "I mean you and <u>MAX</u> saved the day," laughed Grams. "Max," Ali said, touching her nose to his, "maybe Grams can teach you to tap so you can sing AND dance next time!"